When Mom's Away . . .

"Are my girls here?" Mrs. Zucker asked their neighbor.

"Mom!" Caroline, Patricia and Vicki ran to greet their mother in the doorway.

"Give me a second to catch my breath," she said, heading over to the couch. "I have to be back at work in less than an hour, and I could be there all night. A lady from work is going to stay with you."

"Who is this lady from work?" Caroline asked suspiciously.

"Her name is Mrs. Gladstone. She works in the office at the hospital keeping everyone organized," their mother said.

Not another organizer, Caroline thought to herself. She heard enough about getting organized from her mother.

Then she had another thought which made her smile. Mrs. Gladstone wouldn't know the rules at Caroline's house. She wouldn't even know where to find things. They could have a lot of fun confusing an organized person . . . .

Caroline Zucker
Meets Her Match

by Jan Bradford
Illustrated by Marcy Ramsey

Troll Associates

Library of Congress Cataloging-in-Publication Data

Bradford, Jan.
  Caroline Zucker meets her match / by Jan Bradford; illustrated by
Marcy Ramsey.
    p.   cm.
  Summary: When their mother's job takes her away overnight,
Caroline and her younger sisters find themselves stuck with Mrs.
Gladstone, a strict babysitter whom the girls suspect is a witch.
  ISBN 0-8167-2017-7 (lib. bdg.)   ISBN 0-8167-2018-5 (pbk.)
  [1. Babysitters—Fiction. 2. Sisters—Fiction.] I. Ramsey,
Marcy, ill. II. Title.
PZ7.B7228Cau 1991
[Fic]—dc20   90-10813

A TROLL BOOK, published by Troll Associates
Mahwah, NJ 07430

Printed in the United States of America.

10 9 8 7 6 5 4 3 2 1

1

ALL-GIRL WEEKEND

"Dad, will you *please* get me a T-shirt from San Francisco?" Caroline Zucker asked at dinner. "I'd love to have one."

"I'll do my best to get one for you," he promised.

"If they don't have any good ones there, maybe you could check in Los Angeles."

Mr. Zucker laughed. "I'm not going to tour all of California. I'll be too busy at the teachers' conference to get to Los Angeles."

"If she gets a shirt, then I want a San Francisco Forty-Niners hat." Caroline's middle sister Patricia liked to collect hats.

Mrs. Zucker started clearing dishes off the table. "We have to leave in fifteen minutes if we want to get your father to the airport on time."

"Do I have everything on my list?" Mr. Zucker pulled a piece of paper out of his pocket and started to add things to it. "A T-shirt for Caroline. A hat for Patricia. Did you want something, Vicki?"

The five-year-old grinned. "A Mickey Mouse from Disneyland."

He reached across the table to pat her hand. "I'll do my best to bring him home for you."

"What do you want, Mom?" Patricia asked.

"Right now, I want you girls to finish rinsing these plates and put them in the dishwasher. I need to help your father with the last of his packing."

Caroline took her mother's place at the sink while Patricia and Vicki loaded the dishwasher. She couldn't help thinking that her mom had changed. Ever since she had started working as a nurse full-time, she was always talking about being organized. Didn't she know how much fun you could have just doing whatever you wanted to whenever you wanted to do it?

"Look at how big it is!" Patricia pointed through the car window at the plane that was almost above them.

"Is it going to crash on us?" Vicki asked.

"No." Their mother laughed. "The plane is going to land over there."

They all looked out the window as the plane flew lower and lower.

"Will Daddy's plane be that big?" said Vicki.

"Maybe bigger," he told her.

Caroline wondered how something that big got off the ground. She couldn't even jump high enough to reach the granola bars her mother kept on the second shelf in the cupboard. And she only weighed fifty-one pounds.

Their father drove into a parking lot far from the airport terminal building. Everyone got out of the car while he took his suitcase out of the trunk. Then he handed the car keys to their mother.

"Why don't you leave from here?" Mr. Zucker suggested. "You don't all have to come up to the terminal just to say good-bye."

"I want to see you get on the plane," Vicki told her father.

"And I want to ride on the moving sidewalk," cried Patricia.

"I want to go through that thing that beeps," Caroline said.

"Well . . . okay, only if you have empty pockets tonight," her father said with a chuckle.

Last summer Caroline had gone to the airport with her mom when Grandpa Nevelson was going to visit a friend in Canada. A guard made them walk between two posts. When Caroline went through, a beeper sounded. A lady in a uniform hurried over and asked her to take everything out of her pockets—including her magic glow-in-the-dark wizard ring and a box of raisins. When Caroline walked between the posts again, nothing happened . . . but she still smiled when she remembered the fuss she had caused.

They took a bus from the parking lot to the airplane terminal. After Mr. Zucker got

4

checked in and the airline lady put tags on his suitcase, they went to the beeper place.

Caroline went between the posts first and nothing happened. *Rats!* she thought. But the rest of her family still had to walk through. She held her breath as they came toward her one by one . . . but no one beeped, not even a little. How had she been born into such a boring family?

"Hey, Patricia, there it is!" Caroline couldn't walk slowly any longer. She raced ahead and jumped on the moving sidewalk. It was like a flat escalator without steps. Patricia and Vicki were right behind her.

"Hi, Mom!" Vicki waved as their parents walked next to them . . . except they were walking on the regular floor.

"Wouldn't it be neat if we had a moving sidewalk at our school?" Caroline asked. "Wouldn't it be great to ride to lunch?"

"Or the gym," Patricia added.

"Or the bus." Since Vicki only went to half-day kindergarten, she didn't stay for lunch or go to the gym very often.

5

The moving sidewalk ended and the girls stepped onto the non-moving floor.

"This is it," Caroline's father told them as he handed his ticket to a man at the counter.

"Your plane is ready for boarding," the man said.

Mr. Zucker leaned down and said, "That means it's time for me to go."

Vicki threw herself into her father's arms, almost knocking him over. "Don't go, Daddy!"

"I have to go. People are expecting me."

"Then take me with you," she begged.

"I'll bring you a Mickey Mouse," he said to cheer her up.

"I don't want Mickey. I want *you.*"

Their mother untangled Vicki's arms from their father's neck. Then she wrapped her own arms around Vicki and hugged her.

Before Vicki could do anything more to stop him, their father was waving to them from the runway door. Caroline sniffed back a tear and waved. She didn't know why she almost started to cry. Their dad would be home Sunday night. Besides, in only three days she'd

6

have a great San Francisco T-shirt. She should be happy.

They waited until the airplane backed away from the terminal and rolled down the runway and out of sight. Then Mrs. Zucker said, "Let's go. We need to get home and get you ladies into bed. You have school tomorrow."

"Can we stop for ice cream?" Vicki stared up at their mom with her big, brown eyes.

Mrs. Zucker smiled. "I don't see any reason why we shouldn't stop for a treat. After all, we girls are on our own for the next three days."

"Good morning!" their mother said in a happy voice the next day. She was standing at the stove in her robe. "It turned cold last night. I thought oatmeal would taste good today."

"*Real* oatmeal?" Caroline asked. "Not the instant kind? You never have time to make *real* oatmeal."

"I have plenty of time today . . . and tomorrow . . . and the day after that," their mother announced.

The girls stood together in the kitchen doorway and stared. "Is she okay?" Patricia whispered.

"I'm not sure." Caroline studied her mother.

"Don't you have to go to work?" Vicki asked.

"Not until Monday," she told them with a grin. "Today and this weekend are like a little vacation for me."

"Why didn't you tell us before?" Caroline wanted to know.

"I wanted to surprise you." When no one said anything, she asked, "Are you surprised?"

"Yes!" they screamed in unison just before they raced into the kitchen for hugs.

Caroline helped spoon the oatmeal into bowls as their mother described her plans. "This is going to be our very own all-girl weekend!"

"Can we see the new Rocky Bears movie tomorrow?" Vicki begged. They were her favorite cartoon characters.

"If we do that, we should go to Kidstuff Boutique, too," Caroline demanded.

Their mother pulled out her chair at the kitchen table and sat down. "There will be time for everything. And how do you feel about pizza tonight?"

Caroline rubbed her hands together. "Sausage and mushroom?"

"No," Vicki said in her stubborn voice. "Pepper-er-oni."

"It's 'pepperoni,' " Patricia corrected her.

Vicki pouted. "That too."

"We'll get one of each," Mrs. Zucker said.

"It sounds like a party!" Caroline said with a grin.

2

WHERE IS MY MOM?

That afternoon, Caroline ran nearly all the way home from school. She could barely wait for the all-girl weekend to start. As she raced up the driveway, Caroline could see something on the front door. It looked like a piece of paper. Dropping her book bag, she ripped the note off the door. Before she could even read it, Patricia was behind her.

"What does it say?" she asked. "Where's Mom?"

Caroline held the note so Patricia could see it, and then she read out loud: "Caroline and

Patricia—Please go to Mrs. Heppler's house. Vicki is there now. I will explain what's going on as soon as I can. Love, Mom."

"She's gone!" cried Patricia. "She said she would be home, but she's gone!"

Thinking fast, Caroline said, "Mom's not gone. I bet she's just getting ready for our special weekend. What if this is a treasure hunt and the first clue will be at Mrs. Heppler's house?"

"A treasure hunt?" The idea seemed to interest Patricia. "What's the prize?"

"Mom!" Caroline's imagination was running at high speed. "She could have clues waiting for us all around the neighborhood. I bet she's waiting in the car somewhere to take us on an adventure."

Patricia shouted, "Why are we wasting time here? Let's go see what clue Mrs. Heppler has for us."

After looking both ways, they ran across Hawthorne Street. Caroline leaned on Mrs. Heppler's doorbell until the woman opened her door.

"Well, here you are. Vicki and I have been

expecting you," the blond lady told them. "Come on inside."

The girls were surprised to see a plate of cookies and three glasses of lemonade waiting on the kitchen table. Vicki was happily munching a cookie.

"Hi," she grinned. "These are good!"

"Did our mom want us to have a snack here?" Patricia asked before she and Caroline reached for the cookies.

"Actually, it was my idea," Mrs. Heppler said. "I thought you might be hungry after a busy day at school."

Caroline decided that if Mrs. Heppler was part of the treasure hunt, she sure was keeping her secret well. "We'd love to have a snack," she said.

When the girls had finished their lemonade and brushed cookie crumbs off their lips, Caroline asked, "Uh, did my mom leave something here for us?"

Mrs. Heppler shook her head. "She just said she'd be back for you as soon as she could. There was a big explosion at Metro Chemicals this afternoon. Your mom is helping at the hospital. I know she had planned to be home, but the explosion was an emergency. Lots of people were hurt. All the doctors and nurses had to report to the hospital."

"For how long?" Caroline asked.

"As long as they need her," Mrs. Heppler replied. "Hey, do you girls like jigsaw puzzles?"

"If they're not too hard," Vicki said softly.

"I'll help you," Mrs. Heppler promised. She took a puzzle from a shelf in the coat closet. Caroline and Mrs. Heppler helped the younger girls put the puzzle together to make a picture of cuddly kittens in a basket. After a while, they even forgot to be disappointed that their mother wasn't there.

"Are my girls here?" Mrs. Zucker asked Mrs. Heppler about an hour later.

"Mom!" Caroline, Patricia and Vicki ran to greet their mother in the doorway.

"I knew you would come," Vicki told her just before she kissed her on the cheek.

"Give me a second to catch my breath," Mrs. Zucker said. The girls followed her into the living room, where she fell into a soft chair. "It feels so good to sit down."

"Has it been busy at the hospital?" Mrs. Heppler asked.

"It sure has. I'm on my dinner break. I have to be back there in less than an hour, and I could be there all night."

"No, Mom," Patricia argued. "You said you would be home all weekend."

Caroline asked, "Are we going to stay here until morning?"

Their mother smiled. "No, I've made other arrangements. A lady from work is going to stay with you."

They all gazed at their mother in silence. They had never spent the whole night with a stranger.

"Can't you stay home?" Vicki asked in a very small voice.

Mrs. Zucker patted her knee and Vicki hurried to climb into her mother's lap. "I wish I *could* stay home," she told all of them. "But there are people who need my help tonight."

"Who is this lady from work?" Caroline wanted more information.

14

"Her name is Mrs. Gladstone. She works in the office at the hospital keeping everyone organized."

Not another organizer, Caroline thought to herself. Then she had a thought which made her smile. Mrs. Gladstone wouldn't know the rules at their house. She wouldn't even know where to find things. They could have a lot of fun confusing an organized person . . . .

"That sounds just great," she said sweetly.

"Caroline Louise . . . ." Mrs. Zucker narrowed her eyes and stared at her. "If you're making plans, you can just forget them. I work with this lady every day. Please don't embarrass me."

Caroline nodded, but she was very careful not to make any promises.

"Let's all go home and meet Mrs. Gladstone," Mrs. Zucker said. "She's waiting in our living room. Good-bye, Anne, and thanks for helping me in a pinch."

The girls thanked Mrs. Heppler, too, then followed their mother across the street to their own house. Mrs. Zucker opened the door and greeted Mrs. Gladstone. She moved to one

15

side, and without a word, Caroline, Vicki and Patricia inched backwards.

Mrs. Gladstone looked old enough to be a grandmother. Her eyes were dark and almost beady . . . kind of like bird eyes. And there was the most amazing wart on the side of her nose.

Vicki grabbed her mother's skirt.

Caroline knew exactly how her sister felt. Mrs. Gladstone didn't look like a very *friendly* kind of person.

3

YUCK! BRUSSELS SPROUTS!

"And they should all be in bed by nine o'clock," their mother told Mrs. Gladstone, finishing a list of house rules.

The baby sitter nodded as if she were recording each rule in her memory. Caroline got a funny feeling in her stomach that told her it might not be so easy to play tricks on this woman.

Mrs. Zucker kissed each of the girls and then opened the front door. "I'll be here in the morning when you wake up. Remember, I love you!"

The girls waved as their mother hurried down the front steps.

Mrs. Gladstone put her hands in the pockets of her skirt. After she cleared her throat, she surprised them all by saying, "There are two parts to my name, and depending on your behavior I can be like either one. If you're good, I can be glad; if you're not, I can be as hard as a stone."

The girls stood staring at the woman for a moment, taking in her words. Then Patricia spun around and refused to look at her. Vicki just burst into tears. When the baby sitter leaned down to reach for Vicki, the little girl ran to Caroline and threw her arms around her.

"It's okay," she told Vicki. "Patricia and I will take care of you."

"You seem to have everything under control here," Mrs. Gladstone told Caroline. "So I'm going to start dinner."

"I thought we were going to have pizza," Patricia mumbled.

"It's not pizza," Mrs. Gladstone said on her way to the kitchen. "But it's special."

18

She made it sound like a mystery, and that made Caroline curious.

"What do you think she'll make?" she asked her sisters.

"Maybe a roast." Patricia sounded interested for the first time since they had gotten home. "I love when Mom makes a roast with potatoes and carrots."

"She's not Mom," Vicki reminded them.

"Why don't you ask what she's making?" Patricia suggested to Caroline.

"Why me?"

"You're the oldest," Patricia said. Usually Patricia seemed to forget who was the oldest girl in the family. She only remembered when she wanted Caroline to do something.

"Would you girls please put away your school things?" Mrs. Gladstone called from the kitchen.

Caroline picked up her book bag and started toward the stairs. Actually, a mystery dinner could be kind of exciting. Her best friend Maria always said her grandmother made really fun dinners. Maybe they would get lucky.

Maybe Mrs. Gladstone was a nice grandmother in disguise.

"Will you be upstairs long?" Patricia asked. There was a worried frown on her face.

Caroline guessed her sisters didn't want to be alone with Mrs. Gladstone. Feeling very important, she told the other girls, "Wait for me in your room."

Caroline ran up the steps to her attic room. "Hi, Justin and Esmerelda," she called to her goldfish. She threw her book bag on the bed. First, she pulled out the sweater her mother had insisted she wear to school. Since she had taken it off the second her mother couldn't see her, it was perfectly clean. Caroline tucked it into her bottom dresser drawer. Then she took out two books and set them on her desk.

The smell that greeted Caroline on her way downstairs made her nose hurt. What was Mrs. Gladstone doing? Frying worms?

"What's she making?" Patricia asked when Caroline slipped into her room.

"What if it tastes as bad as it smells?" Vicki wanted to know.

They sat around for a while, wondering what

20

dinner could possibly be, before they were interrupted by Mrs. Gladstone.

"Girls!" she called. "Dinner is ready."

They slowly entered the kitchen. It actually smelled worse in there than it had in the bedroom or the living room. Caroline wanted to cover her mouth and nose with her hand, but that would be rude.

Vicki settled into her chair and rested her elbows on her Snoopy place mat. Caroline sat down, eyeing the strange-looking meat on the platter. It was covered with onions, but Mrs. Gladstone hadn't hidden it completely—it was *liver!* Caroline hated liver.

Patricia stood behind her chair with a look of horror on her face. "Brussels sprouts!"

"Sit down!" Caroline hissed. Patricia hated Brussels sprouts as much as Caroline hated liver.

"Take some liver and pass the plate around," Mrs. Gladstone instructed Caroline. "I hope I made enough for you growing girls. I don't eat very big meals myself anymore."

"Uh, Mrs. Gladstone . . ." Caroline tried to think of a way to refuse the liver politely. After

21

all, their mother had asked the girls not to embarrass her by behaving badly. "Could I make peanut butter and jelly sandwiches for my sisters and me instead?"

Mrs. Gladstone blinked her bird eyes. "That's silly."

Maybe she had misunderstood. "I'll do it myself," Caroline explained.

"But there is no need," the baby sitter insisted. "I think we have enough meat and vegetables for the four of us. And liver is so good for you."

After she passed the platter to Patricia, Caroline cut a teeny scrap of meat. Taking a deep breath, she bit into it.

She couldn't do it. No matter how brave she wanted to be, there was no way she was going to eat that liver.

Both Patricia and Vicki tasted their meat. And Caroline could tell from the look in their eyes that they felt the same way she did. They had to do something.

Caroline let her hand drop under her chair and snapped her fingers. It was a signal that her dog Baxter knew well. He hustled into the kitchen and sat next to Caroline's chair.

She waited until Mrs. Gladstone was sipping her coffee before she let a piece of liver drop to the floor. Baxter sniffed at it and then backed away. Now they were really in trouble . . . even Baxter wouldn't eat it!

Still trying to get the liver taste out of her mouth, Caroline drained her glass of milk. What was she going to do without more milk when she had a plate full of liver and Brussels sprouts left to eat?

"Mrs. Gladstone, could I get more milk?"

"Help yourself," she answered, cutting herself a large piece of liver.

As Caroline pushed her chair back, she had a wonderful idea. She cut off a hunk of liver and slipped it into her hand when Mrs. Gladstone wasn't looking . . . but her sisters were. Vicki giggled when Caroline walked over to the refrigerator with the liver in her hand. Before she poured her milk, she tucked the meat behind the pickle jar on the top shelf.

Soon the other two girls finished their milk and hurried to the fridge for refills, too. Caroline knew they couldn't keep getting more to drink . . . Mrs. Gladstone would get suspicious.

Caroline concentrated on cutting the rest of her meat into small pieces that she could push around her plate. If she did it just right, it would look as if she had eaten most of her food. But even after she had hidden a few pieces under her Brussels sprouts, there was still too much left. With a sigh, Caroline rested her elbows on her place mat.

"Caroline, Caroline, strong and able, take your elbows off the table," Mrs. Gladstone lectured.

Caroline laughed at the funny poem. Somehow, she bumped her fork and it fell to the floor. She picked it up and set it on her plate.

Mrs. Gladstone make a clucking noise with her tongue. "You'd better get another one. Although I'm sure your mother keeps everything very clean, you just don't know what that dog has tracked into the kitchen."

Caroline glanced at the three Brussels sprouts on her plate. She could eat one and maybe two. But never three. She had to get rid of one of them. Leaving her right hand in her lap, she reached across her plate with her left one.

She dropped one Brussels sprout into her palm and picked up the fork. Then she dropped the fork into the sink and let the Brussels sprout fall into the silverware drawer.

Mrs. Gladstone finished her dinner soon after the fork trick. She picked up her plate and began to push her chair away from the table. "You girls have done a good job cleaning your plates, so I'll start cleaning up. You're all excused from the table."

"No!" Caroline cried. There was no way that Vicki and Patricia could stand up without dropping the Brusssels sprouts they'd hidden in their napkins. And they would be in *major* trouble if Mrs. Gladstone opened the refrigerator or the silverware drawer.

They had to stop her!

4

NO TELEVISION!

Patricia put on her Miss Helpful face and said, "Since you made the dinner, Mrs. Gladstone, I think it's only fair for us to clean up."

Caroline wanted to kiss her. Her head bobbing up and down in agreement, she added, "Patricia's right."

"Can I rinse?" Vicki asked, almost jumping up from her place at the table. Caroline imagined liver and Brussels sprouts flying everywhere!

Patricia was quick and held Vicki down as she answered, "You can load the dishwasher."

Vicki was too short to reach the sink, so she never got to do the rinsing. For some reason, she seemed to think she was missing all the fun.

"We don't have very many dishes," the baby sitter said. "I hate to think of us wasting electricity. Why don't you wash them in the sink tonight?"

"Sure. We'll wash them. No problem," Caroline said.

"I want to wash!" cried Vicki.

"Well, aren't you girls nice?" Mrs. Gladstone smiled at them. "I think I'll just get my knitting if you don't need my help."

"Go ahead," Caroline said. They all watched her move slowly into the living room. As soon as they heard her knitting needles clicking, Caroline and Patricia raced to throw the rest of their food into the trash bag. After they had added the food Caroline had hidden in the fridge and the drawer, Caroline tied up the bag.

Patricia pulled a chair over to the counter, so Vicki could wash. Her arms were buried in suds up to her elbows. And her big grin was showing off the spaces where she used to have baby teeth.

Caroline grabbed a towel and started wiping a glass that Patricia had just rinsed. "Do you know I'm the fastest dryer in the family?"

"What?" Patricia hated to think anyone was better than she was at anything. She dragged another towel out of a drawer and tried to dry the next glass in less than five seconds.

"Patricia!" Vicki complained, waving a soapy plate in the air. "You're the rinser."

"You can do it yourself." Patricia snatched the last glass before Caroline could get it.

Vicki didn't give up easily. She flicked soap suds at Patricia. "I don't want to do it myself."

Patricia's blue eyes opened wide. "You can't do that to me!" In seconds, her hand was in the dishwater and she was shaking suds at little Vicki.

"Is everything all right in there?" Mrs. Gladstone called from the next room.

Glancing at her sisters, Caroline struggled not to laugh. Vicki had a soapy beard hanging from her chin. And Patricia was speckled with foamy bubbles.

"We're fine!" Vicki and Patricia called before the baby sitter came in to check on them. They decided to end the soap fight. Vicki went back to washing dishes. It didn't take long for them to finish the job.

"I've got an idea," Caroline whispered. "I'm still hungry, so I'm going to make some micro-wave popcorn. You guys go into the family room. I'll bring it in for us."

"Good idea," Patricia whispered. Then she and Vicki tiptoed through the kitchen door that led to the family room.

Caroline heard them turn on the television while she dug in the cupboard for the popcorn. A cartoon theme song was starting in the next room as she lifted one packet out of the box.

"What?"

"You can't *do* that!"

Caroline wondered why her sisters were complaining. Had the television died? With the popcorn packet still in her hand, she trotted into the family room. She couldn't see what was wrong with the television because Mrs. Gladstone was standing in front of it.

"What's happening?" Caroline asked.

30

"I don't think there is any need for television tonight," Mrs. Gladstone said calmly.

In Caroline's opinion, she might as well have told them to stop breathing. "But it's Friday night. We *always* get to watch television on the weekend. Especially when there's a fun cartoon for Vicki." Caroline wasn't going to admit she had been looking forward to watching cartoons, too.

"Tonight will be different." The baby sitter squinted at Caroline and added, "No television, and no junk food."

"If we can't watch TV and we can't eat popcorn . . . " Patricia frowned. " . . . what *can* we do?"

"I think it would be nice if you read or did something else to improve your minds."

Caroline walked back into the kitchen to drop the popcorn back into its box. She and her sisters had very good minds. They didn't need to improve them on a Friday night.

Mrs. Gladstone came into the kitchen. "Your sisters have gone to their rooms to find something to do. Can you find suitable entertainment?"

"Sure." Caroline hurried up the stairs, happy to get away from this horrible woman for a minute. She grabbed her *How to Draw Funny Faces* library book, and then she found paper and markers in her desk drawer.

She tapped the fishbowl to get Justin and Esmerelda's attention. "Are you guys ever lucky. You get to stay up here and do whatever you want."

When she came down the steps, Mrs. Gladstone was checking Vicki's and Patricia's projects.

"These are fine," she told Vicki after she read the titles of her picture books.

Just like a teacher, the woman flipped through Patricia's easy-to-read biography of Beethoven. Personally, Caroline didn't see how reading about a dead musician could improve her sister's mind. But Mrs. Gladstone smiled down on Patricia and said, "This is wonderful."

When Caroline handed over her things, Mrs. Gladstone pursed her lips and shook her head. "This doesn't look very challenging."

"But drawing is hard for me."

Mrs. Gladstone didn't like the excuse. She just shook her head until Caroline ran back up to her room.

"It's me again," she told the fish when she flipped on the light. She dropped the book and her art supplies on her desk. "Mrs. Gladstone is even meaner than my teacher, Mrs. Nicks!"

Caroline wished the fish could say something to make her feel better. Every day she worked so hard at school, hoping Mrs. Nicks would understand she was special. And now Mrs. Gladstone wanted her to study some more!

She could only think of one thing that would please Mrs. Gladstone—her geography homework.

"This is more like it," Mrs. Gladstone said with a teacher-like smile when she saw Caroline's geography assignment.

Together they walked into the living room where the other girls were stretched out on the floor. Vicki was pretending to read the words in her picture books. Patricia was moving her lips as she read her dumb book about Beethoven. Caroline sighed. It looked so boring.

"Is something wrong?" Mrs. Gladstone asked.

She wanted to say, "Yes. I'm hungry and I don't want to do homework tonight." But her mother wanted her to be polite, so she just said, "No—" and hoped that the Zucker all-girl weekend would get better before it was over.

5

MADISON, NEBRASKA?

"Would you like me to read to you?" Mrs. Gladstone asked Vicki.

"Yes." Vicki seemed willing to forget that the woman had tried to make her eat liver. She and Little Pillow, the ragged old pillow she carried everywhere, climbed into Mrs. Gladstone's lap.

In her teacher's voice, Mrs. Gladstone told Vicki, "I like having you sitting in my lap, but we don't need this dirty old pillow, too. Why, it looks as if someone has been chewing on it!"

Without giving Vicki a chance to stop her,

Mrs. Gladstone set her back on the floor. Then she marched into the kitchen and dropped Little Pillow into the trash. Vicki burst into tears.

Mrs. Gladstone hurried into the room and lifted Vicki into her lap again. "Don't cry, honey. I know it's hard to spend the night with a stranger when you're just five years old."

Caroline might have liked Mrs. Gladstone for trying to be nice if she hadn't just thrown Little Pillow in the trash. Sure, she had spent plenty of time wishing her parents would make Vicki give up that old, moldy pillow. But she had never wanted to make her sister sad.

"You have to do something," Patricia whispered.

"It's going to be hard to outsmart General Gladstone," Caroline told her sister.

Patricia giggled. She liked the name. "Then what will we do? Read books all night?"

"I hope not," Caroline said with a groan. "All I know for sure is that all three of us are going to have to stick together."

Somehow Mrs. Gladstone got Vicki to stop crying. As it got quiet, Caroline went back to work on her project.

For her geography homework, Caroline had to fill in states and their capitals on a blank map that Mrs. Nicks had given to everyone in the class.

She started filling in the map with Colorado. Since she lived there, she knew how the state looked on the map. And she knew Denver was the capital.

Two summers ago, they had taken a family driving trip to Nebraska, so she knew it was next to Colorado. They had gone to Omaha, but Omaha wasn't on the city list.

"Madison, Nebraska?" she said to herself, but it didn't sound right. She tried matching other capital cities to the state. "Jackson, Nebraska? Salem, Nebraska?"

Patricia inched closer to her. "What are you doing?"

"My homework." She decided to skip the capital of Nebraska and do Florida. Its capital had a funny name, one that kind of rhymed.

She let her finger slide along the list of city names until she came to it. "Yes! Tallahassee."

"That looks like fun," Patricia said, sounding almost jealous.

"I thought you wanted to read about Beethoven," Caroline teased.

"Well, Beethoven's dead," Patricia said with a sigh. "Can't I help you with your stuff?"

"It's not *stuff*, it's geography," Caroline explained. She couldn't expect her first-grade sister to understand about geography.

"Well, what do you have to do?"

"I have to match the names to the states and then put the right capital city in each state." Caroline hoped Patricia would be impressed with how hard the work could be in third grade.

"Isn't that Michigan?" Patricia pointed to one of the states on the left-hand side of the country.

"I don't think so . . . ." Although Caroline wasn't sure which state was Michigan, she believed the state under Patricia's finger was California.

Patricia squirmed with excitement. "If you don't know, then you can't say I'm wrong. I like this geography stuff."

"I don't want you to like it," Caroline said.

"Why not?"

"Because this is third-grade work. A first-grader can't know all the answers." Caroline could tell her even more things about being in third grade . . . and about being *grown-up*. It meant she had to be nice even if Mrs. Nicks was being mean to her. It meant she had to walk Baxter even on days when it was raining. And tonight it meant trying to take care of her little sisters when Mrs. Gladstone was being strict.

"Girls?" Mrs. Gladstone asked, looking over the top of a picture book. "Are we arguing?"

"No." Caroline wrote *California* inside the state that her sister thought was Michigan. Their father was in San Francisco, California. But San Francisco was not on the city list. Who had decided to make the capitals be cities no one knew about? she wondered.

Starting at the top of the city list, Caroline recognized Atlanta. It belonged in Georgia. But she didn't know which state was Georgia. She twisted her hair while she looked at all the blank parts on her map. Caroline didn't want to look like the dumbest kid in her class. And that is just how she would look if the only states she knew were Colorado, Nebraska, California and Florida.

Her hair was twisted into a tight, smooth knot by the time she gave up worrying about her map. She let it go and watched her hair spring free. It was fun. She decided to twist it even tighter. When she kept turning it around and around, it started to bend into strange shapes. Caroline wished she had a mirror.

"Mrs. Gladstone? I need a bathroom break."

"Heavens. If you need to do that, just go."

Caroline didn't really need to use the bathroom. But she wanted to watch in the big mirror while she played with her hair. Maybe she could bend her twisted hair into animal shapes.

She was on her way to the bathroom when she heard a siren. Baxter jumped up and ran to the front window. He threw back his head and howled.

From her cozy spot in Mrs. Gladstone's lap, Vicki giggled. Patricia set down her Beethoven book and started to laugh. Whenever there were sirens, Baxter seemed to think he was a wolf instead of a half-sheepdog, half-something-else mutt.

Mrs. Gladstone got a funny look on her face. Her bird eyes were narrow and squinting. Her cheeks were turning red. And her right foot was tapping faster and faster on the carpet.

"Quiet!" she demanded. Baxter stopped howling and decided he would rather bark. "You'll have to make him stop that," she told the girls.

The louder Baxter barked, the harder Vicki giggled. And the longer Vicki giggled, the more her sisters laughed.

"This has to stop!" Mrs. Gladstone shouted. "Put the dog in the garage."

Baxter turned away from the window and barked at the baby sitter. He knew what *garage* meant, and he did not want to go there.

When Mrs. Gladstone set Vicki on the floor so she could take care of the dog, Vicki yelled, "Run, Baxter, run!"

Baxter galloped out of the living room.

"Catch him," the woman called to Caroline as Baxter zipped past her.

Caroline raised her hands in the air. "He's too fast."

When Mrs. Gladstone pushed past Caroline to chase him, Baxter ran through the family room and into the kitchen. He went from room to room, making a big circle. No matter how fast she tried to move, Mrs. Gladstone was always one room behind him. When she almost caught up with him, Patricia and Caroline got in her way. Of course, they pretended they were trying to help her catch the dog.

A stair creaked and both girls knew exactly where Baxter had gone.

"I think he must have gone into Vicki's and my room," Patricia told Mrs. Gladstone innocently.

As soon as the baby sitter peeked into the room, all three girls ran upstairs. Baxter was sitting in the middle of Caroline's room. His tail started to wag as soon as he saw them.

"Poor Baxter." Vicki patted him on the head. "We won't let her put you in the garage."

He whined when she mentioned that horrible place.

They heard the step squeak and Patricia turned to Caroline. "She's coming!"

"Baxter, under the bed," Caroline told him. Patricia lifted up the edge of the bedspread. He didn't move.

"Is that dog up here?" Mrs. Gladstone called from just outside the door.

At the sound of her voice, Baxter took the girls' advice and tried to squeeze under the bed. But he was a big dog and Caroline's bed was pretty close to the floor. He couldn't quite fit in the space. So the girls lined up next to the bed to hide him.

Mrs. Gladstone stood in the open doorway, trying to catch her breath. When she found her voice again, she said, "Nice try, girls. But I can see his tail."

Caroline glanced down and saw Baxter's tail sticking out from under her bedspread. "But Mrs. Gladstone, he *hates* the garage. I think he's afraid of the dark."

"He's a dog, not a baby." Mrs. Gladstone took two steps into the room.

To everyone's surprise, Baxter pushed his head out between Vicki's and Patricia's legs.

He was showing his teeth! When Mrs. Gladstone took one more step toward him, he snapped at her!

"He doesn't bite," Caroline said. "At least, he never has before . . . ."

"Well, I don't want to be the first person he bites." Mrs. Gladstone went back to the doorway. "Let's make a deal. The beast can stay in the house, if he keeps out of my sight."

Since Baxter couldn't speak for himself, the girls answered for him. "It's a deal!"

6

PEANUT BUTTER AND MARSHMALLOWS

"I'm so *hungry*," Vicki complained after Mrs. Gladstone went back to her knitting.

"Me, too." Patricia put her hand on her almost empty stomach.

The answer seemed simple to Caroline. "Then we need to get some food."

Patricia shook her head. "Mrs. Gladstone won't let us have any snacks."

"Of course she won't." That little problem didn't bother Caroline. "We'll just have to sneak downstairs, steal the food, and eat it up here."

46

"What if she wants us to stay back down-stairs?" Vicki asked.

"I can take care of General Gladstone," Caroline told them. She went to the top of the stairs and called, "Mrs. Gladstone . . ."

The woman came to the bottom of the stairs, still holding her knitting. "Yes, Caroline?"

"Could we stay up in my room? We want to make a present for our mom."

The General smiled. "Isn't that sweet? Yes, you can do that, dear."

Dear. Caroline shivered on her way back to her room. She didn't want the General to call her *dear.*

"Who's going down first?" Vicki asked.

"I am," Caroline volunteered. "In case I get caught, I can say I'm looking for something we need to make Mom's present."

She went down the stairs slowly, being very careful not to let the noisy step squeak. When she reached the bottom, she peeked at Mrs. Gladstone. The baby sitter was knitting and humming along with some song playing on the radio.

Caroline held her breath and tiptoed into the

47

family room and then into the kitchen. The first thing she did was take Little Pillow out of the trash can. Then Caroline went to work. First, she scooped a handful of cookies out of the cookie jar. Next, she found some crackers, peanut butter and a knife. The bag of marshmallows behind the peanut butter jar looked very good, so she grabbed that, too.

She set all the food in the center of Little Pillow and wrapped the edges around it. With the pillow ball pressed to her stomach, Caroline started her dangerous trip back to her bedroom. She tiptoed through the family room and flattened herself against the hall wall so Mrs. Gladstone couldn't see her. Then she ran up the stairs, jumping over the squeaky step.

"What are you doing?" she cried when she saw her markers and paper spread out all over her bed.

"We wanted it to look like we're really making something in case Mrs. Gladstone comes up here," Patricia explained.

"Good thinking." Caroline pushed aside a few markers and dropped the goodies on the bed.

"Little Pillow!" Vicki sounded so happy that Caroline thought she might start crying again. Instead, Vicki pulled her pillow out from under all the food. Crackers and cookies flew in every direction.

"Marshmallows!" Patricia ripped open the bag like a starving person. Then she stuffed a handful of the mini-marshmallows into her mouth.

Caroline reached for the crackers and the knife. "Would you like some peanut butter?" she asked Vicki.

Her little sister was hugging Little Pillow so hard that feathers were popping through the holes and fluttering to the floor. "Yes, please."

For once, Caroline did not complain about Little Pillow leaking feathers. She felt all warm inside, knowing how happy she had made her sister.

She spread peanut butter on a few crackers and handed two to Vicki. Her stomach was begging for food, so she kept the other crackers for herself.

Patricia found a cookie that had landed on Caroline's teddy bear. She said, "Excuse me,

Mr. Bear. But I want this more than you do."
She bit into her chocolate chip cookie. "Ooh.
It's soggy."

"Sorry. Try some peanut butter on it," Caroline suggested. She wiped the knife over the cookie, leaving a peanut butter glob in the middle of it.

Just one bite made Patricia gag. "I need something to drink!"

"There's soda in the fridge," Caroline thought out loud. "But I was afraid the General might hear me open the door."

"We need to keep her busy," Patricia said.

Caroline picked up a green marker and scribbled on a sheet of paper. "I'll ask the General for some help with this picture while you get the soda," she told Patricia.

"What about me?" Vicki was still holding onto Little Pillow.

"You should stay here and . . . watch Baxter. We have to keep him away from Mrs. Gladstone," Caroline said.

Vicki grinned. She was proud to have an important job.

The tricky step squeaked when both girls

51

walked on it at the same time. "Get behind me, so Mrs. Gladstone won't see you," Caroline whispered.

Patricia made a big deal about sneaking into the family room. What did she think she was? Caroline wondered. A real burglar?

"Mrs. Gladstone?" Caroline said, trying to sound sweet and *dear.* "Could you help me?"

The woman looked up from her knitting. "I can try."

Taking a deep breath, Caroline sat on the couch next to the baby sitter. She handed over her sheet of paper. "We're trying to draw a nice flower. Patricia can make a good rose, but none of us can do the leaves."

Mrs. Gladstone bit her lip to keep from laughing when she saw Caroline's attempt to draw a stem with leaves. "I guess you weren't kidding before when you told me you couldn't draw."

Mrs. Gladstone took the green marker from Caroline and quickly added a few lines to each side of the scribble. To Caroline's amazement, the woman really did turn the mess into a flower stem with leaves.

"Hey, that's neat!" Caroline said, forgetting to watch for Patricia. She heard something that sounded like a hiss. Glancing over her shoulder, she saw her sister peeking around the corner.

Caroline moved even closer to the General, blocking the woman's view of the stairs. "Could you show me how you did that?" she asked the baby sitter.

"It's not hard," Mrs. Gladstone said. "You just needed to straighten out this line, and then make a few curved lines come out on each side."

The step creaked under Patricia's foot and Caroline coughed to cover the noise. She listened for her bedroom door to open and close and then she took back her paper.

"Thanks, Mrs. Gladstone. This will really fix our picture."

"I was glad to help," the woman said. "But you'd better work fast. It's almost time for bed."

"All right." Caroline ran as fast as she could.

Patricia and Vicki were both snapping open their soda cans when Caroline raced into the room. "She said it's almost bedtime. We have to eat fast."

They didn't talk for the next five minutes. Patricia ate the rest of the marshmallows. Caroline choked down her can of soda and then finished the box of crackers. That left only soggy cookies for Vicki, but she seemed to like them with peanut butter on top.

The squeaky step warned them Mrs. Gladstone was coming upstairs. Caroline hurried to hide the food. The empty cracker box and peanut-butter jar were slipped under her bedspread. She pushed the soda cans under her bed. Vicki jumped onto the bed, hiding Little Pillow beneath her.

Mrs. Gladstone opened the door without even knocking. "Time to start getting ready for bed."

Vicki groaned and Caroline noticed her baby sister was looking kind of green. Maybe the cookies had been bad. Or maybe she had had too much root beer.

"I feel—"

Before Vicki could say she felt sick, Caroline gave her a big hug and said, "She's so tired."

"Then a hot bath should feel good." Mrs. Gladstone took Vicki's hand and led her out of the room.

Caroline and Patricia followed them downstairs. When they peeked into the bathroom, Mrs. Gladstone was adding bubble stuff to the water and she was saying the strangest thing.

"Water and soap make fun bubbles. Down the drain go all the troubles."

Mrs. Gladstone stood up. "Why don't you girls go upstairs and clean up the mess in Caroline's room? But Patricia, be back here in fifteen minutes for your bath."

"The mess?" Caroline repeated as they went up the steps. "Was she talking about the markers and stuff, or did she see the food?"

"I don't know." Patricia sounded as worried as Caroline felt. What if she knew what they had done? Would she tell their mom?

In exactly fifteen minutes, the General called for Patricia. While the second bath was happening, Caroline sneaked Little Pillow back into Vicki's room.

"Is that you, Caroline?" Mrs. Gladstone called.

"Yes." She glanced at the clock in Vicki's room. Patricia's bath had lasted exactly fifteen minutes, too. The bath schedule was strange, but what happened next was totally weird. After Caroline's bath, the General called, "Everyone to the bathroom."

She had set their toothbrushes out in a row. And there was a glob of green toothpaste on each of them. The girls filed into the bathroom and each stood by her own toothbrush.

Mrs. Gladstone checked her watch. "You will start brushing when I say *go,* and you will brush for five minutes."

"Five minutes!" Caroline cried. She didn't have enough teeth to brush for five minutes.

"Five minutes," the General repeated. She squinted at her watch. "Okay. Ready, set, go!"

Caroline realized the woman was serious. The General was going to stand there and watch them brush their teeth for *five whole minutes!*

The next time she saw her mother, Caroline was going to ask her if Mrs. Gladstone really had been in the army.

7

THERE'S A WITCH IN MY HOUSE!

"Weird, weird, weird," Caroline muttered as she walked into her room. Mrs. Gladstone was downstairs, tucking the other girls into bed.

"There is something strange about that woman," she told her goldfish. "I don't know exactly what it is. First, she tries to starve us. Then she was really nice about the picture. But she was really creepy about baths and teeth brushing." Caroline tucked her geography assignment into the notebook on her desk. She couldn't stop thinking about the General. She just wasn't like a real baby sitter.

When Grandpa Nevelson stayed at their house, he told them funny stories. And Laurie Morrell, the high-school girl who watched them in the afternoon until one of their parents came home, was fun, too. She let them bake things and make a mess in the kitchen. Sometimes she rented movies and they watched them on the VCR.

"Maybe we've just been lucky to have baby sitters like Grandpa and Laurie," she told the fish.

She walked over to the fishbowl and watched Justin and Esmerelda swim around in a circle. "I know she's my mom's friend. But guys, I don't like her!"

Caroline didn't hear her door open. But suddenly Mrs. Gladstone was there. Had she been listening?

"Time for bed," she said. What had she heard? Did she care?

Caroline climbed into her bed. It was full of cracker crumbs! But they had to stay her secret. She pulled her sheet and blanket up under her chin and tried to ignore the scratchy leftovers.

With a pretend smile, she said, "Good night, Mrs. Gladstone."

"Good night, Caroline. Sleep well." She closed the door, leaving Caroline in the dark.

With no one to see her except maybe Justin and Esmerelda—if goldfish could see in the dark—Caroline sat up in bed and saluted. "Yes sir, General Gladstone!"

Caroline was almost asleep when she thought she heard something. She turned her head and saw her bedroom door opening.

Who—or what—was sneaking into her room? Was the General coming to get her? Had she noticed the soda cans under her bed? Or the cracker box sticking out from under her bedspread?

"Caroline?" Patricia whispered, shining her flashlight in her sister's face.

When she realized it was Patricia, Caroline sighed with relief. "Of course it's me. Who else would be in my room?"

"Shh!" Vicki followed Patricia. She stopped to close the door. Then both girls hopped up on Caroline's bed, burying their feet under the folded-back bedspread.

Patricia turned off her flashlight. "Vicki thinks Mrs. Gladstone is a witch," she whispered.

"A *what?*" cried Caroline.

"A witch," Vicki said for herself.

"I think it's stupid," Patricia announced. "I told her she should listen to me."

"How do you know she's wrong?" Caroline asked. When she thought about it a little longer, she had to add, "It *would* be exciting...."

The more she thought about it, the better it sounded. She loved adventures. How many people could say they had a real witch in their house? Maria, her best friend, was never going to believe it. Caroline had to be sure, before sharing the story, that it was true. So she told her sisters, "We'll have to *prove* Mrs. Gladstone's a witch."

"How do we do that?" Patricia said.

Caroline tried to remember all she knew about witches. "What about *The Wizard of Oz?* What happened to those witches?"

"A house fell on one," Vicki remembered.

"And the other one melted when Dorothy threw a bucket of water on her," Patricia said. "Mrs. Gladstone put her hand in Vicki's bath water, and nothing happened to her."

"That doesn't mean she's not a witch," Caroline insisted. "They're probably not all the same. What about that strange poem she said about the bath water?"

"And she tried to poison us with liver," Vicki added.

Patricia agreed. "That was really gross."

"Don't forget Baxter." Caroline was beginning to believe Vicki was right. "He's never snapped at anyone . . . except Mrs. Gladstone."

"And what about the wart on her nose?" Vicki asked. "She even *looks* like a Halloween witch!"

Patricia laughed. "That doesn't prove anything."

"I suppose you're right." Caroline fell back on her pillow. There had to be some other way for them to know if their baby sitter was a witch.

"Grandpa told us a witch story once . . . ." Vicki said at last.

62

Caroline knew which story Vicki was remembering. "When he was a forest ranger, he and his partner saw something odd in a cabin one night. When they looked in the window, they saw witches inside—they were chanting something and dancing around lighted candles on the floor."

"You believe that?" Patricia asked.

"I think so," Caroline answered. "Of all his stories, I believe his forest ranger ones the most."

"Me, too," Vicki added.

"Shh . . . ." When her sisters were quiet, Caroline listened carefully for any noise downstairs. "I think I hear something."

They could hear a steady drumbeat.

"Do you think she's dancing?" Vicki whispered.

They each tried to imagine Mrs. Gladstone dancing in a circle around some candles. And they all started to laugh.

Caroline said, "We have to find out what's happening down there. Someone has to sneak downstairs and spy on her."

"Let Vicki do it," Patricia said. "She's the one who thinks Mrs. Gladstone is a witch."

"She can't," Caroline said. "She's too little."

"Of course I can," said Vicki. "I'm brave. Can I, Caroline?"

"Maybe." Caroline knew Vicki was very good at slipping around the house without being noticed when she wanted to be sneaky. "Will you be careful?" she asked Vicki.

Vicki was very serious when she answered, "Yes."

"And you'll come right back here as soon as you see something?"

Vicki put on her flashlight to show she was holding her right hand over her heart. "I promise." In a second, she was starting down the steps.

8

HOW CAN WE ESCAPE?

"Why are we sitting in the dark?" Patricia asked after Vicki closed the door behind her.

"I don't know." Caroline turned on the small reading lamp next to her bed.

Patricia folded her hands in her lap. "She's not going to find anything. It's silly for us to sit here and wait for her."

"Maybe the General will be sneaking a liver and onion sandwich and she'll invite Vicki to have some with her," Caroline suggested.

"Vicki should be downstairs by now," Patricia said.

"Maybe Mrs. Gladstone is playing our video games—"

Patricia dove toward Caroline and stole her pillow. Not giving her sister a chance to think, she hit her over the head. "You're crazy. She's not playing video games."

Caroline used her teddy bear to protect herself from Patricia's next attack. "Then what if Mrs. Gladstone is dancing around lighted candles in our living room?"

Patricia tried to hit her sister again, but this time Caroline grabbed one end of her pillow and held onto it.

Patricia pushed herself down to the foot of Caroline's bed. "Keep your dumb pillow."

Knowing how much Patricia hated being wrong, Caroline was careful when she asked, "What if Vicki is right? What are we supposed to do?"

"Vicki is playing make-believe," Patricia insisted.

"But if she isn't, we have to decide what to do. We can't really spend the night in a house with a witch."

"Why not? Maybe she'll teach us a few tricks," Patricia teased.

"Or maybe she'll put a spell on us . . . " Caroline swallowed hard and could see a change in Patricia's expression, too. "How can we keep her away from us?"

"I don't know." Suddenly, Patricia was whispering.

Caroline knew she had to be responsible since she was the oldest. "I think we might have to leave."

"Where would we go? It's dark outside!" Patricia hugged her knees to her chest.

"We'd go to someone's house," Caroline said. "Mrs. Heppler is nice, and she knows Mom is working. She wouldn't ask too many questions in the middle of the night."

"Okay. But how are we going to get there? If Mrs. Gladstone *is* a witch, do you think she'll let us walk out the front door?" Patricia asked.

Caroline had to admit Patricia had a point. One person could sneak around, but if they tried to escape as a group, Mrs. Gladstone would be sure to hear them. "How about tying my sheets together and climbing out my window?"

"I'm afraid of heights," Patricia said. "I don't want to climb out on the roof or anything. I hope Mrs. Gladstone really isn't a witch."

"We should know soon." Caroline glanced at her clock. "Vicki's been gone for too many minutes. She should be back by now!"

"What could have happened to her?" Patricia asked.

Suddenly, Caroline's hand flew to her heart when she thought of something else. "What if Mrs. Gladstone put a spell on Vicki?"

Patricia gasped. "We have to save her!"

They nearly tripped each other when they both jumped off the bed at the same instant. Patricia fell over Baxter, who had decided to sleep next to the bed. Caroline grabbed Patricia's arm and caught her before she could hit the floor and make a lot of noise.

They moved slowly and quietly as they left Caroline's bedroom. Before they reached the bottom of the staircase, the noisy step groaned. Baxter was coming to help them. Personally, Caroline was happy to have his company.

When all three of them finally reached the bottom of the staircase, they peeked into the living room. It was empty. Caroline looked around the room. Mrs. Gladstone's knitting was lying on the couch. But there were no candles.

"I'll check the downstairs bedrooms," Patricia said.

"Good idea." Caroline rubbed her hands together and said quietly, "I'll look in the kitchen and the family room."

Patricia had taken a few steps toward the bedrooms before Caroline started into the kitchen. Her heart nearly stopped beating when she heard her little sister's voice.

"It hurts." Vicki was crying so hard, Caroline couldn't understand what she said next. Then she cried, "Make it stop!"

"Hush, little darling," Mrs. Gladstone said in a soft voice.

Patricia must have heard the crying, too. She and Baxter nearly ran into Caroline as they all raced through the kitchen.

They slid across the kitchen tiles and ended up at the open doorway to the family room.

69

Mrs. Gladstone was rocking gently back and forth in Mrs. Zucker's chair. Vicki was wrapped tightly in her arms. Her sister's little shoulders were shaking, so Caroline knew Vicki was still crying. What had that awful woman done to her?

9

MRS. GLADSTONE KNOWS EVERYTHING

"Let go of my sister!" Caroline demanded. She sounded much braver than she actually felt.

"Put her down!" Patricia added.

"*Ruff!*" Baxter wanted to help, too.

Mrs. Gladstone rubbed Vicki's back and gazed at Caroline, Patricia and the dog. Very slowly, she said, "I am not a witch."

"Uh-oh," Patricia said under her breath.

Caroline gasped. Vicki had told Mrs. Gladstone they thought she was a witch!

Caroline narrowed her eyes and stared at the

baby sitter. "If you're not a witch, why is Vicki crying?"

"Come over here so we can talk," Mrs. Gladstone told them.

Caroline stepped into the room, but stayed as far away from the woman as she could. Patricia and Baxter hid behind her.

"Vicki is crying because she stubbed her toe in the dark kitchen," the baby sitter explained. "You know, girls, sneaking around in the night can be dangerous. Do you believe me?" Mrs. Gladstone asked them, still rocking Vicki. "Do you believe I'm not a witch?"

"I believe you," Patricia said suddenly. She pushed past Caroline and walked to the center of the room. "I never really thought you were a witch. It was a stupid idea."

Caroline frowned at her sister. She wasn't totally convinced. She still had one more question.

"If you're not a witch, what was that thing you said before Vicki's bath?" The more she thought about the silly poem, the more it sounded like a chant or a spell.

"What did I say?" Mrs. Gladstone seemed

72

confused. Vicki whispered something and the baby sitter laughed out loud. "Are you talking about 'Water and soap make fun bubbles, down the drain go all the troubles'?"

"That's it! What does it all mean?" Caroline said, sounding as tough as she could.

"It's just something I used to say when my children were little—"

"You have *children?*" Caroline asked, amazed.

Mrs. Gladstone chuckled. "My children are all grown now. But when they were little, they used to hate taking baths, so I made up that poem for them."

"Oh." Caroline felt silly. Staring at the floor, she finally said, "I guess you're not a witch."

Patricia clapped her hands. "Real smart, Caroline. It took you long enough to figure it out."

"Be nice to Caroline," Vicki said, speaking for the first time.

"She's right," Mrs. Gladstone told Patricia. "Your sister was doing what she thought was best for you."

Baxter sighed and flopped down on the floor. All the excitement had made him tired.

"Do you all want to go back to bed, or would you like to stay up a little longer?" Mrs. Gladstone asked.

"Stay up!" they cried all at once.

"Then why don't you get that old pillow for Vicki?" she told Patricia. "I think she misses her little friend."

Patricia glanced at Caroline. Were they going to admit they had already gotten it out of the trash can?

"But I thought you threw the pillow away," Patricia said, trying to sound innocent.

"And you girls got it back for her. It's probably in her room," the baby sitter suggested. "And Caroline, would you like to make hot chocolate for everyone? Or do you have an upset stomach?"

"My stomach is fine."

"You didn't get sick from the cookies and crackers and peanut butter?"

Caroline's mouth fell open. "Did Vicki tell you about that, too?"

"She didn't have to tell me," Mrs. Gladstone explained. "When I came up to your room, I saw the crumbs and the cracker box . . . and

74

there's a little bit of peanut butter on your rug. I'll help you get the spot out in the morning. Your mother won't have to know about it."

"Really?" Caroline was starting to forget why she had nicknamed Mrs. Gladstone the General. "Can I ask you something?"

The baby sitter pulled a tissue out of her pocket and wiped Vicki's nose. "Of course, dear."

"If you knew we took back Little Pillow . . . and you also knew we were eating up in my room . . . why didn't you get mad at us?"

"You weren't hurting anything." Mrs. Gladstone gazed down at little Vicki and smiled. "It's not as if you were writing on the walls or jumping on the furniture."

Caroline blinked. Was she dreaming? A little while ago, she was convinced the baby sitter was a witch. Now, she looked more like a nice, old grandmother.

"If you feel all right, Caroline, could we have that hot chocolate?"

"Sure, Mrs. Gladstone." Caroline went into the kitchen and found the packets in the cupboard. "Four hot chocolates coming up!"

She was still waiting for the drinks to be ready when she heard the drumbeat—the same one they had heard upstairs when they thought Mrs. Gladstone was dancing. Only now, she could hear jungle-like music, too. Caroline ran back into the family room. "What is that music?"

Mrs. Gladstone pointed to the television. She was watching a movie! "Do you like Tarzan, Caroline?"

"Uh . . . sure. Were you watching this about . . . half an hour ago?" If she had been watching the movie earlier, why hadn't Caroline and Patricia heard the television when they came down to find Vicki?

"The movie has been on for over an hour. I just turned the sound off when Vicki got hurt." She hugged Vicki close to her and pretended to be telling Caroline a secret. "I don't think your little sister likes Tarzan very much."

Ping. "It sounds like hot chocolate time," Mrs. Gladstone said when she heard the buzzer.

Five minutes later they were relaxing in the family room. The girls were sitting on the floor while Mrs. Gladstone rocked in their mother's chair. The hot chocolate tasted good, but it would have tasted better if there had been some marshmallows left.

"I was surprised when Vicki told me you all thought I was a witch," Mrs. Gladstone told them. "I didn't mean to scare anyone."

"I guess we never had a baby sitter like you before." Caroline knew it wasn't a great excuse, but it was the best one she had. Now that they knew Mrs. Gladstone was a nice lady, it was hard to explain why they had thought bad things about her.

"I didn't know that you had never eaten liver before." The woman laughed. "I made my children eat it at least once a month. I wonder if they thought I was as mean as a witch on those days."

"And my bath was too short," Vicki told her. "I didn't have time to play with Denny Duck."

The complaint didn't bother Mrs. Gladstone at all. She just said, "There are so many things I have forgotten about children."

"Tell us about your children," Patricia sug-

77

gested. "What was it like when they were little?"

Mrs. Gladstone rocked back in her chair and looked off into space. "Well . . . the world was very different thirty years ago. We didn't watch television nearly as much as people do now. And the grocery stores weren't full of so many snack foods. I guess I was thinking you girls needed to eat better and read more . . . ."

"I *like* to read," Caroline told her.

"I read a lot," Patricia said, trying to sound as smart as Caroline.

Vicki didn't want to be left out, so she said, "I'm going to learn to read soon."

Patricia made slurping sounds as she tried to get the last drops of hot chocolate out of her cup, but Mrs. Gladstone just smiled. Whenever they made noise with their food, Laurie Morrell teased them. She told them they should learn to have better manners, or else they were going to be very embarrassed on their first date.

Mrs. Gladstone got out of her chair and started to collect the empty cups. Caroline jumped to her feet. "I can do that."

"That's very nice." Mrs. Gladstone handed her cup to Caroline and went back to her chair. "I like you girls. I especially like the way you take care of each other."

As Caroline walked into the kitchen, she heard Vicki say, "I love my sisters."

Patricia and Caroline both knew they should say something nice about each other, but it was hard. It wasn't that Caroline didn't love Patricia, but she didn't like talking about it.

"I know you all love each other," Mrs. Gladstone said to save the others from getting embarrassed.

The Tarzan movie ended, and the announcer said *Late Night Horror* would be starting in a few minutes. Patricia said, "Can we stay up to see it? Please . . . ?"

Mrs. Gladstone frowned. "I think you're too young for that."

Patricia moaned.

"But if you want to be scared . . ." Mrs. Gladstone laughed in a creepy way like someone in a horror movie. " . . . I can tell ghost stories."

"Yes!" Vicki jumped up and down. "Tell us one."

79

"Let's get our flashlights," Caroline told her sisters. "Then we can turn off all the lights in here."

"We need pillows, too!" Patricia was already on her feet.

A few minutes later, all three girls were cuddled together at Mrs. Gladstone's feet. Vicki and Patricia were lying on the floor with their heads on their pillows. Caroline sat up and hugged her pillow. Vicki pointed her Mickey Mouse flashlight at Mrs. Gladstone's face when she started to talk.

"Once there was a house in the mountains. It wasn't just *any* house. There was a secret room under the stairs . . . ."

10

THERE'S A GHOST AT MY WINDOW!

Mrs. Gladstone reached up and hit the light switch. "That's it, girls. Time for bed."

"Just one more," Patricia begged.

"But I've told you six stories. It's very late."

"She's right." Caroline yawned. Listening to ghost stories had been fun—especially when Patricia put her flashlight under her chin and made herself look scary. But it was time for them to get some sleep.

"Do we have to brush our teeth again?" Vicki asked.

"For five minutes?" Patricia added.

"You should . . . there was sugar in the hot chocolate."

Vicki put on her sweetest face. "We won't tell our mom."

"All right." Mrs. Gladstone smiled. "To bed with all of you."

"I'll let Baxter out," Caroline volunteered after Vicki and Patricia had gone to bed. Baxter knew what the word *out* meant. He raced her to the back door.

"I can wait for him," Mrs. Gladstone offered from the kitchen.

"It's okay." Baxter didn't stay out long at night. He hated it when his feet got cold.

A minute later, Baxter hurried into the house. He looked from Mrs. Gladstone to Caroline and then he sighed.

"He's looking for my mom or dad," Caroline explained. "He usually sleeps on the floor in their room."

"He can still sleep in there. I won't mind having him in the same room if he stays off the bed," Mrs. Gladstone said.

Caroline patted Baxter and bent down to kiss

his shaggy head. "Good night, Baxter. Good night, Mrs. Gladstone."

"Sweet dreams," Mrs. Gladstone told Caroline, checking that the back door was locked for the night. "We'll have a big breakfast in the morning . . . and I promise, no liver."

Caroline stumbled up the steps to her room, but when she opened her door, she thought she was in the wrong place. Both Patricia and Vicki were cuddled in her bed.

Patricia sat up. "We thought you might be afraid to sleep alone after all those scary stories."

"I wouldn't be alone." Caroline picked her old teddy bear off the floor. "I have a friend."

"Now you have two *more* friends," Vicki said cheerfully.

"But my bed isn't big enough for three people." Caroline had tried sleeping with Vicki once before. Her littlest sister rolled around in the night and kicked a lot.

"But we're small," Patricia reminded her.

Caroline could tell she was not going to get her sisters out of her bed before morning. She hopped onto the nearest side and told Vicki, "Move over."

"What was that?" Patricia whispered a few minutes later.

"I didn't hear anything," Caroline told her.

"It sounds like someone's scratching on a window. Listen!"

They all held their breath, waiting for the sound to come again. Suddenly, there was a shrieking noise outside and Caroline dove under the covers.

"Someone is out there." Vicki did something she had not done for a long time. She started to suck her thumb.

"They're crying," Patricia said.

Caroline said, "I thought they were yelling."

When the shrieking noise came again, they jumped out of bed and ran down the stairs, dragging their pillows and blankets behind them.

"What . . . ?" Mrs. Gladstone cried when the three girls jumped onto her bed.

"It's horrible!" Patricia told her.

"A ghost is upstairs," Vicki said, her eyes as big as fifty-cent pieces.

Mrs. Gladstone rubbed her face and turned to Caroline. "What happened?"

"We were all in my bed, and we kept hearing noises. First, someone was scratching at my window. And then we heard another person . . . or thing . . . *screaming,*" Caroline said.

Mrs. Gladstone chuckled. "I'm sure it was just the wind. Aren't there trees outside the front window?"

"Yes," Caroline answered.

"So the scratching noise was simply a branch brushing against a window," Mrs. Gladstone explained.

But that didn't answer all their questions. Caroline asked, "What about the screaming?"

"The crying," Patricia insisted.

"It was probably the wind." Mrs. Gladstone tried to smooth her hair into place. "The wind can sound spooky in the middle of the night."

"Can we stay here anyway?" Patricia asked.

"Yes. Please . . . ." Vicki begged.

With a big sigh, Mrs. Gladstone threw back the blankets. "Anyone who wants to sleep here tonight has ten seconds to get under the covers."

The girls shouted and climbed into the bed. Their legs tangled together in one big knot, and they were squirming around to get their legs free when Mrs. Gladstone yelled, "Ouch!"

"I'm sorry," Patricia said quickly. "I didn't mean to kick you."

"I'll be all right. But I think you girls need to settle down."

"We will," Caroline promised. And she really meant to stop fooling around . . . until Vicki turned on her flashlight under the covers.

She put the light in her ear and whispered, "Is it coming out my mouth?"

"What? The light?" Patricia asked.

"Of course it isn't. You have bones and things between your ear and your mouth," Caroline explained.

Vicki pouted. "How should I know? I'm only in kindergarten."

"Give me the flashlight," Patricia told her. She held the light under her hand. "Look. You can almost see through my skin . . . ."

"What about *your* bones and things?" Vicki wanted to know.

Patricia put her face close to Vicki. "I don't *have* bones. I'm made of *jelly*."

"You are not!" Even Vicki didn't believe that silly story.

"Hush, girls," Mrs. Gladstone scolded. "Even if you're not tired, I need to get some sleep."

Caroline and her sisters held their breath. In the silence, they heard another sound.

"What was that?" Patricia whispered.

"It sounded like someone at our front door . . . ." Caroline's heart was beating double time. "Mrs. Gladstone, someone is trying to break into our house!"

"Nonsense," the woman mumbled. She sounded half asleep. "It's just the wind."

Caroline wished she could believe Mrs. Gladstone. But only a person could be trying to turn the doorknob.

"I'm scared," Vicki whispered.

The front door creaked. Mrs. Gladstone sat up in bed.

"Did you hear that, too?" Caroline asked, but it was hard for her to talk. She was almost too scared to think.

All of them heard footsteps coming toward

the bedroom. Caroline reached out for her sisters and they all held hands. Mrs. Gladstone leaned over the edge of the bed for the phone.

"I'm calling nine-one-one," she told them.

"I hope they're fast!" Caroline cried when a shadow fell on the wall outside the open bedroom door.

Patricia screamed and they all scrambled to hide themselves under the blanket. The older girls pushed Vicki to the foot of the bed, where she would be safest.

"What is going on here?"

All three girls struggled out from under the blanket and jumped to the floor. *Mom!*"

Mrs. Zucker stood in the doorway. She turned on the light switch and checked her watch. "Why aren't you in bed?"

"We were," Vicki said with a grin.

"We were sleeping with Mrs. Gladstone," Caroline explained.

"It was too scary to stay alone," Patricia told their mother.

Mrs. Zucker sat on the corner of the bed. "It looks like you had quite a party here."

"It wasn't exactly a party," Mrs. Gladstone

told their mother. Her cheeks were a little pink, and Caroline wondered if she was embarrassed. It was as if they had all been caught misbehaving.

"We heard noises up in Caroline's room, so we had to come down here," Patricia said, trying to help Mrs. Gladstone explain what had happened.

"We didn't imagine everything. Some of it was real," Caroline said. "Like when we heard you opening the front door . . . except we didn't know it was you."

"That was the scariest," Patricia told her.

"But then you were home." Vicki looked very pleased that their mother was back where she belonged.

"Yes." Mrs. Zucker opened her arms and gave each of them a hug. "And now that I'm home, I want you to go to bed in your own rooms. *Alone.*"

They took turns getting their good-night kisses. Then their mother told them, "Sleep well so we can have a good time with what's left of our all-girl weekend . . . starting tomorrow morning."

"Pizza!" Patricia licked her lips.

Vicki clapped her hands. "The Rocky Bears movie!"

"Kidstuff Boutique!" Caroline added.

"Good night, Mom. Good night, Mrs. Gladstone," the girls called as they carried their pillows and blankets into the hall.

Behind her, Caroline heard her mother talking to Mrs. Gladstone. "I thought I'd come home and find everyone sleeping. But, no . . . ." Her mom chuckled. "The way you make everyone behave at the hospital, I thought you'd keep my girls in line."

Caroline ran back into the room. "Don't be mad at her, Mom. We had lots of fun."

"How much fun?" her mother asked with a smile.

"*Tons.* Can Mrs. Gladstone stay with us again the next time you have to work all night?"